PARIS

PARIS

with
PRIVATEERS

RONALD FRAME

faber and faber
LONDON · BOSTON

First published in 1987 by
Faber and Faber Limited
3 Queen Square London WC1N 3AU

Photoset by Wilmaset Birkenhead Wirral
Printed in Great Britain by
Redwood Burn Ltd Trowbridge Wiltshire
All rights reserved

British Library Cataloguing in Publication Data

Frame, Ronald
Paris *and* Privateers
I. Title
822'.914   PR6056.R262
ISBN 0–571–14776–3

CONTENTS

FOREWORD

I have to admit, it seemed to me the least likely of several ideas I took to producer Tom Kinninmont and his script-editor Marilyn Imrie: a tale about two elderly unmarried women on shrinking pensions who *do* very little, two strangers who accidentally make one another's acquaintance and embark on a verbal relationship that consists (in uncertain proportions) of memories and confected fables about their pasts. . . . But Tom and Marilyn, wholly to their credit, were of quite another opinion, and saw much more in it than I was able to.

I had already published a ten-page short story called 'Paris', whose sole characters are two genteel spinster ladies of restricted means living in the West End of Glasgow. They've both been retired from work for several years: one was a teacher in a private boys' school until she reached the official age of 'handing over' to someone younger, and the other was formerly a buyer of high-quality fashion garments in an up-market store ignominiously razed to the ground by bulldozers at the tail end of the 1960s. The schoolteacher has continued to lament no longer having a focus for her maternal concerns, while the fashion buyer is still unable to adjust to her loss of status: from what seem to be their distant poles of experience, they both view the neglect of 'standards' in the 1970s and 1980s with a common alarm and sorrow.

My two characters were fairly clear to me: what they *did* in the short story – visits to tea-rooms and art galleries and, at a later point, to a cinema – mattered only for the opportunities permitted me to draw *them* out of themselves. As usual in my stories – even if the admission is presumptuous-sounding – I wanted to locate the inner life, with all its manifold contradictions. Complementing that in a way, their physical appearance is what they glimpse in mirrors or reflected in shop windows or the glass inside picture frames, the hazardous manner in which their private selves attempt to engage with the busy, sceptical, narrow-eyed world in the streets. In my short story they're described as speaking – they're forever talking to one another, each about her own life as it was and might have been – but I hadn't in fact provided them with any specific dialogue between quotation marks.

To state the most glaringly obvious, what a television script is, is *dialogue*: and so in that respect I now found myself having to start from scratch. In the process I also learned that, even more importantly, a script requires a controlling *idea* (the element of 'vision' that carries the story forward), plus all the many directions and asides necessary to inform actors, cameramen and technicians. To my initial surprise (I had presumed it must be the director's job) I was asked to provide the general movements and (let's call them) attitudes as well as the words of my characters, to 'see' and choreograph each scene from its start to its finish. Bit by bit, as we worked, the dialogue seemed to be whittled down, which I felt rather guilty about: after all, wasn't I being paid to put the words into my characters' mouths? In time, that came to bother me much less as the inessential was removed and separate speeches were dovetailed together: the dialogue became spare and parsimonious, taut and tight, and I realized that the characters of fiction on the screen will assert themselves, as in life, by a multitude of other indicators: by their silences, by facial expressions, by bodily evasions, by little self-betraying tics one doesn't need to decode.

In toto I supplied four drafts of a script. Marilyn, Tom and I discussed each of them in great detail, more or less line by line. Drafts 2, 3 and 4 each involved me in a fortnight's concentrated work, and were begun as soon after the last script session as I could manage. Naturally enough, I wanted to do my rewriting before I started to forget the details of our discussion. There's also the distinct danger of an idea – or your enthusiasm for it – slipping from you, and I didn't care to take the risk. No doubt the miserable Calvinist work ethic played its part too – don't shirk, there's a job to be done/you're being paid for this/look for problems if they don't already exist, distrust anything that comes too easily – but that is a long and absurd story. . . Three times the play was unstitched and re-operated on, until at last the professionals – Tom and Marilyn – felt confident we had a version we were able to go with.

I count myself very fortunate that we secured the services of two such intelligent and practised and disciplined actresses for our leads as Jean Anderson and Noel Dyson. I had hardly given them the easiest of briefs – each was playing a woman who lived on whichever plane of perception suited the moment – but they debated the nuances in each new scene as we came to it with fine insight and exemplary enthusiasm and dedication to the project. (I'd like to acknowledge how appropriately dressed Misses Nesbit and McLeod were, by costume designer David Beeton: as the women's personalities redefined themselves, so did their choice of clothes subtly alter.)

I was doubly fortunate in working with such patient and sympathetic colleagues as Marilyn and Tom. For me it was a very welcome break in routine to exchange the solitude of prose-writing for the much more sociable business of script sessions. My script-editor provided a female angle on events and my producer/director a male, and I was the point of synthesis, as it were. I learned that the act of so-called 'creative' writing (or should I call it 'destruct-ive'? – but that's another long and complex story, best kept for another time) need not be lonely and claustrophobic.

Novels and short stories, however decently reviewed, reach comparatively few people. I enjoy writing for radio, where the same sort of intimacy is possible between teller and hearer as between writer and reader. Television is the most democratic and challenging medium: by a prose-writer's standards there's a hypothetically huge audience of lookers-in, and it's my purpose and obligation to hold their attention from one scene to the next to the next. Perhaps some of that audience seldom pick up a book, and this has to be my Big Chance. As I see it, they're giving me a unique commodity, a gift of their time: in return I want to entertain of course, but I also want to do a little more – to nudge them, to cause them to consider their assumptions (or at any rate to bring them to recognize that they have such things), to make them not forget the programme the moment it fades from the screen, to seed a few memories of what they've just seen.

Knowing that an audience is there and has to be kept watching concentrates *my* attention wonderfully well. How to attend to the task in hand, though? By – I suggest – being as *honest* as possible: honest to the way people's minds work. Our situations are all different but the differences needn't defeat us: in writing this play I meant to show that there's something of Miss Nesbit and Miss McLeod in every one of us. A lie declares a truth about the person who is compelled to speak it; we all live between rigorous, unmendable 'truth' and our chosen interpretations, our preferred, selective fictions.

I don't write to make political points, or to be circumstantially 'relevant' in the social sense. The best I can hope for, how I justify myself, is to try to induce an awareness of what merits our sympathy and understanding in lives that may otherwise appear utterly distinct and apart from our own. The purpose is as wide – but, I trust, not as vague or abstract – as (ahem!) 'Humanity'. As yet I haven't got very far, if I ever shall or *can*. 'Paris' was an attempt at a beginning.

R.F.

PARIS
A play for television

Paris was first shown on BBC Television on 25 June 1985. The cast was as follows:

MISS MCLEOD	Jean Anderson
MISS NESBIT	Noel Dyson
MRS BLACK	Eileen McCallum
FRENCH WAITRESS	Susie Maguire
WOMAN IN PATISSERIE	Sheila Latimer

Produced and directed by	Tom Kinninmont
Designer	Guthrie Hutton

EXT. PATISSERIE, GLASGOW: DAY I
MISS MCLEOD *enters the patisserie.*

EXT. PATISSERIE: DAY I
MISS NESBIT, *standing on opposite pavement. Traffic passes
between her and the camera.* MISS NESBIT *appears anxious. A
break occurs in the traffic;* MISS NESBIT *moves across Byres Road.
She pauses in front of the patisserie window, adjusts collar and cuffs.
Opens handbag, puts on reading glasses. Reads bill of fare. Takes
off reading glasses.*

INT. PATISSERIE: DAY I
MISS NESBIT *pushes door open and enters. She focuses on the room
inside as she drops the spectacles into her handbag. She's wearing a
turban and a fitted winter overcoat; she's on the brink of being
overdressed. She advances towards table where* MISS MCLEOD *is
sitting.*
WAITRESS: (*To* MISS NESBIT) Bonjour.
MISS NESBIT: May I?
   (MISS MCLEOD *is dressed in moss-coloured tweeds, with a dun
   scarf and brooch. She looks up, taking in the elegant, slightly
   outmoded presence of* MISS NESBIT *as best she can.*)
MISS MCLEOD: I'm sorry?
MISS NESBIT: May I? Join you?
MISS MCLEOD: Oh. Yes. Yes, of course.
MISS NESBIT: I'll never get used to the cold in Glasgow.
MISS MCLEOD: How long have you been here?
MISS NESBIT: Thirty-two years.
   (MISS MCLEOD *moves her chair over;* MISS NESBIT *lowers
   herself regally on to hers.* WAITRESS (*obviously French*)
   *appears from behind counter. She is rather sallow, pert; obliging
   – but just and no more; indeed, verging on disdainful at several
   points. She serves cake and tea to* MISS MCLEOD.)

WAITRESS: (*To* MISS MCLEOD) Bon appétit! (*Offering menu to* MISS NESBIT, *now seated.*) Madame?

MISS NESBIT: I've forgotten my reading glasses. A cup of your coffee please, dear.

WAITRESS: (*Unimpressed by the play's first untruth, since she's already seen* MISS NESBIT *enter*) Café noir? Café au lait? Espresso? Capuccino?

MISS NESBIT: (*Removing gloves*) Café au lait, if you please. (WAITRESS *has turned her back before* MISS NESBIT *has quite finished.*)

MISS NESBIT: (*Noticing cake*) That looks rather good.

MISS MCLEOD: You don't mind if I begin?

MISS NESBIT: A moment on the lips. A lifetime on the hips. Not that you need to worry. (*Air of awkwardness between the two women for a few moments.* MISS MCLEOD *begins — cautiously — to eat.* MISS NESBIT *looks in direction of the cake counter.*) What should I have? Just for a treat? What would you recommend? I haven't been here before —

MISS MCLEOD: (*Laying down pastry fork*) No. I haven't either. (*Hesitates.*) The tarte aux pommes is nice.

MISS NESBIT: (*Doubtfully*) Y-e-s.

MISS MCLEOD: They've one with cherries too. (WAITRESS *brings coffee to* MISS NESBIT.)

WAITRESS: (*To* MISS NESBIT) Café au lait. You would like to eat something, madame?

MISS NESBIT: Yes. The cake with cherries, please, dear.

WAITRESS: Cerises?

MISS NESBIT: If you'd be so kind — (*The two women look nonplussed by waitress's lack of grace.* WAITRESS *makes her return with plate, containing cake. The plate is offered, somewhat unceremoniously, to* MISS NESBIT.)

MISS MCLEOD: (*Lowering her voice*) She's French —

MISS NESBIT: (*The words have 'depths'*) That explains it, then.

WAITRESS: Bon appétit!

MISS NESBIT: (*Watching* WAITRESS'*s back*) A smile, we used to say, costs nothing . . . (*Pause.* MISS NESBIT *regards cake.*)

MISS MCLEOD: (*Hazarding*) They put them in brandy, don't
   they? The French?
MISS NESBIT: (*Looking puzzled*) Begging your pardon?
MISS MCLEOD: (*Slightly tongue-tied*) Cherries. Because they're
   out of season, I mean.
   (*Pause.* MISS NESBIT *turns plate, inspects her tart.*)
MISS NESBIT: I just like the colour. On a winter's morning. I've
   an eye for colour. (*Pause.*) When I was in business we used
   to buy ourselves a cake on Friday afternoon, as a reward for
   being good girls all week.
MISS MCLEOD: Yield not to temptation for yielding is sin.
   (MISS NESBIT *puts Sweetex in coffee.*)
MISS NESBIT: I used to work in London. Regent Street. Then
   Piccadilly.
MISS MCLEOD: You come from London?
MISS NESBIT: (*Suggestion of evasiveness*) Originally. London
   way. I was on the buying side. High quality garments.
   Then I came up to Glasgow. I had my own department.
WAITRESS: (*Serving cup of coffee to* MISS NESBIT) Bon appétit,
   madame!
   (MISS NESBIT *eyes the sullen girl.*)
MISS NESBIT: I'd tell her she *had* to smile.
MISS MCLEOD: (*Looks at girl, then turns to* MISS NESBIT) The
   waitress? Maybe she's a wee bit off colour?
MISS NESBIT: We had to, in business – smile. (*Smiles, grimaces
   rather.*) Whether we felt like it or not. Well, there were days
   like that, weren't there? You know – ? (*Nods meaningfully.*)
MISS MCLEOD: (*Studies plate, then ventures the word*) Yes.
   (*Looks up, towards* MISS NESBIT.)
   (*Pause.*)
MISS NESBIT: What about yourself?
MISS MCLEOD: (*Taking a second or two to recover from previous
   'admission'*) Oh, I'm from Glasgow. Hyndland. I – taught.
   Boys. In the preparatory department.
MISS NESBIT: 'To Serve Them All Your Days – '
MISS MCLEOD: Yes, I suppose so.
MISS NESBIT: Did you see that on television?

MISS MCLEOD: I don't watch awfully much –

MISS NESBIT: We've both 'served'. In our different ways.
    (*The women look at the* WAITRESS, *who's standing behind the
    counter. She's smoking. Blue cigarette packet.* MISS MCLEOD
    watches MISS NESBIT'*s close attention.*)

MISS MCLEOD: Probably she's from Paris.

MISS NESBIT: Paris? (*She raises eyebrows.*)
    (*Pause.*)

MISS MCLEOD: Have you been?
    (MISS NESBIT'*s attention turns back to* MISS MCLEOD.)
    To Paris?

MISS NESBIT: Me? No. Have you?

MISS MCLEOD: No.
    (*Pause. We're conscious of the 'ethnic' background music.
    Again we view the girl smoking.* MISS NESBIT *extracts a
    cigarette from her handbag and secures it firmly in a holder.*)

MISS NESBIT: (*Recovering some of her impetus*) I always meant to.
    I *could* have gone to the Collections. The fashion shows, in
    September. For 'business'. Still . . . I suppose it's nice to
    think about some things, isn't it? Plan. What you *might* do if
    you went there. (*Pause.*) The stores would have been worth
    seeing. (*Pause – exhales cigarette smoke.*) You don't mind?
    (MISS MCLEOD *tilts her head.*)
    My smoking?

MISS MCLEOD: (*Speaking too quickly*) No. No.

MISS NESBIT: It's not a proper *vice*, is it? It's a treat. To hell
    with the expense! (*Pause.*) Now, what was I going to say?
    What were we talking about?

MISS MCLEOD: Paris –

MISS NESBIT: Oh, yes.

MISS MCLEOD: The shops –

MISS NESBIT: (*Crossing arms on table top*) Well, I had a good
    friend, Miss Carmichael – she was in business too, for
    another store, in Buchanan Street – we *talked* about going
    to Paris, one year when we would both be free.
    (*Pause.*)

MISS MCLEOD: (*Hazarding*) Why didn't you – ?

MISS NESBIT: (*She's been looking towards the window and the door. She turns to* MISS MCLEOD.) Oh. She was a bit – 'pernickety', isn't that the Scotch word? (*Exhales.*) She said it could be dangerous. For women. Outside Notre Dame men follow you about. You can't sit down there.
MISS MCLEOD: I didn't know.
MISS NESBIT: (*With a worldly expression*) It's the same on some of the boulevards. You have to know which ones are safe. Montmartre, of course, it's – what's the expression? they use it on the television news all the time? – it's a 'no-go' area. 'Ladies of pleasure'.
MISS MCLEOD: (*Awed by the information*) I didn't realize. I mean, I've read –
MISS NESBIT: Well, it's not *all* like that, of course –
MISS MCLEOD: (*Anxious to save Paris's good name*) I'd like to see the galleries. The Jeu de Paume, where the Impressionists are. (*Sees a confusion building on* MISS NESBIT'*s face.*) The Impressionist painters. The Jeu de Paume, in the Tuileries Gardens.
(*Pause.*)
MISS NESBIT: Yes, and there's the Louvre. The Mona Lisa.
MISS MCLEOD: Oh, yes.
(MISS NESBIT *sips at coffee.*)
MISS NESBIT: It's expensive, this French coffee. But it's worth it.
(MISS MCLEOD *eats a forkful of her cake.* MISS NESBIT *puts down her cup. Now she seeks her own 'ground'. She spies the flower in the glass vase on the table; she holds up the vase.*) Isn't that a picture? Don't you think?
MISS MCLEOD: It's lovely.
MISS NESBIT: (*Authoritatively*) Soft colours are very good for a pale skin. Flattering. (*Considering* MISS MCLEOD, *assessing.*) It would suit *you.*
MISS MCLEOD: (*Surprised – but also interested*) Me?
MISS NESBIT: (*Looking from flower to* MISS MCLEOD) Of course, mossy colours are very – discreet.
MISS MCLEOD: (*Surprised*) Oh, I've always worn them.

(*Pause.*)
So, if they see me –

MISS NESBIT: If they see you – ? Who?

MISS MCLEOD: The boys I taught. I'll seem the same to them –

MISS NESBIT: (*Not understanding fully*) They'll recognize you?

MISS MCLEOD: (*Repeating*) Yes, they'll recognize me. (*Finding her original meaning*) They'll see I haven't changed.

MISS NESBIT: (*Appearing sceptical, changing tack, with more than a hint of irony*) 'A woman ages into character and elegance.' That should be her motto. You ought to try a hyacinth pink. It's so sympathetic to a light complexion. My friend Miss Carmichael was a great devotee of soft pink, 'to make the boys wink', she would say.

MISS MCLEOD: I don't think I could wear a modern colour.

MISS NESBIT: That kind of pink isn't. It's timeless. I don't like strident colours nowadays. Colours should be subtle, and tone well. Don't you think? . . . Think pink . . .

MISS MCLEOD: I don't really know terribly much about – colour. I like paintings. That kind of 'colour'. Reading about paintings. (*Attempting a joke*) But *I'm* not an oil painting . . .

MISS NESBIT: (*Self-mockingly*) 'The customer is whoever and however she imagines herself to be.' Miss Nesbit's rule.

EXT. UNIVERSITY AVENUE: DAY I
Shot of two women from behind. MISS MCLEOD *is wearing sensible, flat shoes.* MISS NESBIT, *while wearing nothing remotely outlandish on her feet, is having some difficulty in walking.*

MISS NESBIT: (*Acknowledging the awkwardness, doing her best to 'laugh it off'*) You wouldn't believe it, I had to teach the girls – the mannequins – how to walk. We had shows in the store. With an orchestra.

MISS MCLEOD: Yes. I remember. Glasgow had style then.

MISS NESBIT: Of course, it's changed days now.

(*Shot of two women making their way uphill, towards the Hunterian. The two women slow as they approach the building.*)

– I – (*Rather winded*) *I'm* going up here.

MISS MCLEOD: (*Shivering; fastening on façade of Mackintosh House*) Have you ever been into the House?

MISS NESBIT: (*Taking advantage of the pause to get her breath back*) The 'House'?

(*Shot of exterior of Mackintosh House.*)

MISS MCLEOD: The Charles Rennie Mackintosh House, they've rebuilt it in there.

(*The two women look up at the façade of the building.*)

MISS NESBIT: Have *you*?

(MISS MCLEOD *shakes her head.*)

MISS MCLEOD: I've always meant to go.

(MISS NESBIT *tips cuff back, looks at her watch.*)

MISS MCLEOD: I don't think you pay in the mornings.

MISS NESBIT: (*Suddenly looking attentive; sounding decisive*) Well . . . let's go in, then. (*Cheerfully*) It'll be a new experience. (*Pause.*)

(*With a smile*) By the way – I'm Dorothy Nesbit.

MISS MCLEOD: (*A little more hesitantly*) Jean – McLeod. (*Parting shot of the two standing shaking hands.*)

INT. CHARLES RENNIE MACKINTOSH HOUSE, WHITE ROOM: DAY I

MISS MCLEOD: I *do* like Art Nouveau. That whole *fin-de-siècle* period. Don't you? In Vienna they thought Mackintosh was a genius.

MISS NESBIT: How did you learn?

MISS MCLEOD: Learn?

MISS NESBIT: About Art-y things?

MISS MCLEOD: I – had a friend. A close friend. We went to galleries. Alistair and I. A long time ago.

MISS NESBIT: It sounds very romantic.

(*Pause.*)

Like that advertisement on television, you know, where the woman and man bump into each other in front of a picture. (*Pause.*)

You with your 'Alistair'.

MISS MCLEOD: (*Being lured into the deceit*) With Alistair? Yes, I
suppose it was – 'romantic' –
(*Shot of* STUDENT *inside white drawing-room of Mackintosh
House; she's very 'artily' dressed, and is sketching.* MISS
NESBIT *can't resist scrutinizing the girl, and she loses the
subject of 'Alistair' for a while. Both women walk slowly
around the furniture.*)

MISS NESBIT: (*Lowering her voice only marginally*) Now women
don't seem to bother how they look. How they present
themselves.

MISS MCLEOD: It *costs* so much.

MISS NESBIT: Don't tell me! (*Pause.*) The people who have money
nowadays weren't educated for it. Of course, I always 'knew'
– in my line of 'business'. As soon as someone stepped into the
department. I could tell by how I was treated, you see. You
had to let them know, some of them. It had started in those
days, some people coming up and others going down.

MISS MCLEOD: It changed at the school too.
(*We see these two women as historically 'isolated'. Spectral
quality of light we remember later in snow scenes. Art student
tears off page from notepad, begins to sketch rapidly. Through
next sequence of shots, occasional cuts to student sketching.*)

MISS NESBIT: How long did you teach there?

MISS MCLEOD: Till I retired. (*Pause while she calculates and
works up to the 'admission'.*) Thirty-seven years. One
hundred and eleven terms.
(*Pause.*)

MISS NESBIT: Have you seen *The Prime of Miss Jean Brodie?*
(*After her disclosure,* MISS MCLEOD *is looking rather lost.*)
The film? With Maggie Smith? She had lovely clothes, Miss
Jean Brodie. She had a love affair with the art master.
Robert Stephens.
(MISS MCLEOD *nods, but without appearing to comprehend.*)
She had a 'set'. The 'Jean Brodie Set'. She told her girls
they were 'the *crème de la crème*'.

MISS MCLEOD: (*Somewhat hesitantly*) I think – it's wrong – to
have favourites . . .

MISS NESBIT: Men were wild for her. The art master was. She
    was terribly 'modern'.
MISS MCLEOD: (*Struck by a possibility*) Do I remind you of her?
MISS NESBIT: Well, I don't know *what* you got up to in the Art
    Department! Do I?
    (*Pause – till the reply comes. When* MISS MCLEOD *does speak,
    there's a note of helplessness in her voice.*)
MISS MCLEOD: All that was out of my hands.
MISS NESBIT: You had the hard graft?
MISS MCLEOD: (*We catch a sense of frustration*) I taught boys to
    be disciplined.
MISS NESBIT: Disciplined?
MISS MCLEOD: To work hard. To know their own capabilities.
MISS NESBIT: (*Not catching the undertow of frustration*) 'My name
    is Jean McLeod – and I'm in my prime.'
MISS MCLEOD: (*Asking the question as much of herself as of*
    MISS NESBIT) I wonder if you know when you're 'in your
    prime'?
MISS NESBIT: Oh, the best is yet to come!

EXT. CHARLES RENNIE MACKINTOSH HOUSE: DAY I
MISS NESBIT: How are you placed for Wednesday?
MISS MCLEOD: (*Brightening*) Next Wednesday? We could go
    back to the patisserie. If you like – ?
MISS NESBIT: Yes. Yes, I *should* like –

INT. PATISSERIE: DAY 2
*A blackboard menu should be reasonably conspicuous in the
background, behind the seated women.* MISS NESBIT *is dressed
differently,* MISS MCLEOD *isn't.*
MISS NESBIT: (*Savouring the atmosphere. Still wearing coat but
    removing her turban*) I *could* go. (*She looks round.*) To Paris.
    I'd love to try one of those tourist boats with the open tops.
MISS MCLEOD: Bateaux-mouches.
MISS NESBIT: Brigitte Bardot was on television, being
    interviewed on one.
MISS MCLEOD: I didn't see that.

MISS NESBIT: She's fifty, Bardot. She's a miracle.

MISS MCLEOD: (*Nodding*) Walking round the Louvre –

MISS NESBIT: (*Enjoying the game*) The cafés. Sitting out on the pavement.

MISS MCLEOD: Someone sent me a postcard of the Palais-Royal once. The arcades and the fountains. Colette lived there. (MISS NESBIT *appears not to know if she should recognize the name.*) The writer. With her cats.

MISS NESBIT: Ah, that's one of the things that's kept me from going, you see. I've a cat. *He*'s got a French name – 'Pissarro' –

MISS MCLEOD: (*Mildly shocked*) I beg your pardon? Like the painter?

MISS NESBIT: I inherited him. And the name.

MISS MCLEOD: From an art-lover?

MISS NESBIT: Not from a cat-lover, anyway. (*Laughs.*) From someone at business. In millinery.

MISS MCLEOD: Why didn't you change his name?

MISS NESBIT: I thought he seemed rather a wicked cat. Well, he hadn't been trained. House-trained, I mean. I just kept the name.

MISS MCLEOD: They've got some of his pictures here, in the Art Galleries.
(*Pause.*)

MISS NESBIT: We *should* go.

MISS MCLEOD: Where? (*Astonished.*) Paris?

MISS NESBIT: No, the Art Galleries. Places like that. Cultural places. Where your man friend took you.

MISS MCLEOD: Yes.

MISS NESBIT: (*Brightfully, hopefully*) I've so much catching up to do. We could go to the Burrell Gallery. (*Breathing in on her cigarette in its holder*) I love a day out. Miss Carmichael and I used to go to the cinema. I like French films best. The women have such style. Jeanne Moreau. Catherine Deneuve.

MISS MCLEOD: I don't know their names.

MISS NESBIT: Deneuve's very beautiful. Rather icy, blonde. (*Pause. Scrutinizing* MISS MCLEOD, *setting her head at an angle.*) Have you ever dyed your hair?

MISS MCLEOD: (*Seeming rather baffled*) Dyed my hair?

MISS NESBIT: But I don't suppose you needed to –

MISS MCLEOD: (*Simply*) Boys always see through what is not – true.
(*Pause – Miss Nesbit's smoke passes across the table.*)
I don't think I should have been true if I'd dyed my hair.

MISS NESBIT: Once you'd started, though – (*Decides to drop the topic.*) Oh well . . .

MISS MCLEOD: Is your hair – ?

MISS NESBIT: I use a colour rinse. I do it myself. It's just as good as a salon would do it.

MISS MCLEOD: I wouldn't have guessed. About the rinse, I mean.

MISS NESBIT: That's the point. You shouldn't be able to.

MISS MCLEOD: Does it really matter if you do? Guess?

MISS NESBIT: It means you should get another colour rinse!
(*Pause. An uncomfortable feeling that* MISS NESBIT *has provided a ticking-off.*)

MISS NESBIT: (*Appeasing*) Were you very strict?

MISS MCLEOD: (*Automatically*) Boys respect discipline.

MISS NESBIT: Wasn't that a strain?

MISS MCLEOD: A strain?

MISS NESBIT: Having all those rules? Caps on in the street.

MISS MCLEOD: We Scots are a very disciplined race. It's in our nature.

MISS NESBIT: (*Intrigued; also an element of prurience*) Did you – cane them?

MISS MCLEOD: (*Carefully, deliberately*) Sometimes it was necessary.

MISS NESBIT: Spare the rod and spoil the child.
(*Pause –* MISS MCLEOD *considers the table top.*)

MISS MCLEOD: You have to behave well.

MISS NESBIT: (*Tilting her head. In a tone that could possibly be construed as disparaging*) Caps on in the street? Ties knotted?

MISS MCLEOD: (*Raising her eyes to* MISS NESBIT. *More than a hint of defensiveness*) Yes. You should dress not to offend people: not to make them embarrassed. Boys – men – should know to open a door for a member of the opposite sex. (*Self-justifying.*) That kind of thing. You don't ever forget.

MISS NESBIT: So I'll know one of your boys if I meet one? He'll open a door for me?

WAITRESS: More coffee? (*She pours from the jug of coffee on the table into Miss Nesbit's and Miss McLeod's cups.* MISS MCLEOD *looks away.* MISS NESBIT *repositions the cigarette in its holder.*)
(*After attending to neighbouring table. The remark seems to go unheard by the two women.*) Bon appétit!
(*Shot of* MISS MCLEOD *glancing round the room and of* MISS NESBIT *beside her, studying her.*)

MISS NESBIT: (*Curious. We should hear the friendliness – even care? – in her tone*) Who are you looking for?

MISS MCLEOD: (*She doesn't appear unduly pathetic as she says this: she's an independent woman, and yet we are conscious of a certain frailty, a vulnerability. She says such things with a quiet dignity that allows her our sympathy, she's anything but ridiculous*) I always think I'll see someone. Someone I taught. Or they'll see me.

MISS NESBIT: Do they?

MISS MCLEOD: Sometimes. I think so. (*Her eye alights on the blackboard. A 'professional' look appears on her face: eyes intent, lips drawn together. There is not quite a shake of the head; echo of a little triumph in her voice.*) They've mis-spelt 'profiteroles'.

MISS NESBIT: (*Making an effort of p-e-e-r-i-n-g into the distance*) Where? Have they? I haven't brought my reading glasses.
(MISS MCLEOD *gets to her feet. She walks over to the blackboard, corrects mistake by rubbing out an additional letter in the word, a second 'R'.*)

MISS MCLEOD: (*With satisfaction of a task accomplished*) That's better.

MISS NESBIT: (*Silently applauding; a satisfaction too in her
companion's boldness, which we should appreciate has been less
than automatic instinct*) Jean Brodie would have been proud.
(MISS MCLEOD *sits down at the table; she smiles bashfully,
recognizing her sudden status of heroism. We should have the
sense that a closer rapport is now possible. Pause. The two
women sit sipping coffee.*)
MISS MCLEOD: (*Buoyed up, aiming the question gently; she's
interested to know the answer*) Don't you – ever wish you'd
stayed in London?
MISS NESBIT: (*Shrugs*) Water under the bridge.
(*Pause. Apparently* MISS MCLEOD *is warming to a revelation
as she takes another sip of her coffee and watches* MISS
NESBIT. *Simultaneously the* WAITRESS *saunters past. She
places a French-style stainless steel domed sugar bowl on the
table.* MISS NESBIT *passes the girl a particularly glazed smile;
she studies her clothes.*)
(*Eyes still on girl*) Is *she* from Paris?
MISS MCLEOD: I think so.
MISS NESBIT: She looks art-y.
(MISS MCLEOD *is watching the girl and making her own
mental associations.*)
MISS MCLEOD: My grandfather trained in Paris. He was an
artist. He used to say there was a 'silver light' there.
MISS NESBIT: (*Turning back to* MISS MCLEOD) Do you
remember much about him?
MISS MCLEOD: He died when I was young. He had a grey bushy
beard.
MISS NESBIT: Whereabouts did he live?
MISS MCLEOD: Kirkcudbright.
MISS NESBIT: No, in Paris?
MISS MCLEOD: Oh. On the Left Bank. Near the Jardin du
Luxembourg. The Sorbonne part. Very bohemian –
MISS NESBIT: The Left Bank! I'd love to have gone! The names
have such romance! (*Gulps on cigarette.*) I had it planned
with Miss Carmichael, we'd even booked it. The Left
Bank, a little hotel. Blossom-time. I'd bought a spring

costume . . . We were going to treat ourselves. (*Looks at cigarette in holder, then at* MISS MCLEOD; *then with a mixture of confidence and matter-of-factness.*) I 'lost' her. (*Clicks her fingers.*) Just like that.

MISS MCLEOD: (*With apparent concern*) Oh, I'm sorry –

MISS NESBIT: No, I mean she married. Same thing. We had to cancel the trip. She married a man her own age – a widower – he manufactures ball-bearings. They live in Largs.

MISS MCLEOD: Is she happy?

MISS NESBIT: She told me she was. (*Pause.*) Still, it was a turn-up for the books. At our – at the age she was. (*Tidies loose strands of hair.*) You can't expect it.

MISS MCLEOD: No.

MISS NESBIT: You give up thinking of that, don't you?

MISS MCLEOD: Yes. You do.

MISS NESBIT: I think she was just 'lucky' really.

MISS MCLEOD: Getting married?

MISS NESBIT: *Finding* a husband. Such a comfortably off one. (*Without much conviction*) I *believe* she's happy.

MISS MCLEOD: Yes. (*Rather limply*) Well, I'm sure she is. (*Pause – the two women might look at each other's dress.*) (*Quietly.*) My friend at school, Miss Davie, *I* lost *her*. She went back to the Mearns. Her 'calf-country', she called it. She had a little cottage with a garden. (*Sense of story tailing away.*)

MISS NESBIT: (*After a discreet pause*) Is *she* happy; your friend?

MISS MCLEOD: (*Cautiously*) I don't know. We wrote to each other at first. Her garden takes up her time. She didn't like to talk about the school too much. It was as if she'd forgotten . . .

MISS NESBIT: (*A heavy 'theatrical' sigh*) C'est la vie!

MISS MCLEOD: (*With a discreet but sad smile*) C'est la vie! (*Pause. The two women stoop forward to their cups and sip.* MISS MCLEOD *seems to relish its warmth.* MISS NESBIT *sits back, inhales and exhales, her eyes attending to* MISS MCLEOD *through the blue fog.*)

MISS MCLEOD: (*Looking into cup; pleasure of the moment, also vague undertow of sadness?*) One could get to like this French coffee. It's rather unusual. I wish I'd known about it sooner.

MISS NESBIT: It's expensive – but it's worth it, I think.
(*Pause.*)
They put chicory in it, the French. You shouldn't touch coffee, of course, it's so bad for you.

MISS MCLEOD: Balzac used to drink it. Night after night after night. It poisoned him.

MISS NESBIT: We're just having a treat.
(*Pause –* MISS NESBIT *lights up another cigarette, leans back in her chair. Today she is being 'brave' . . .* MISS MCLEOD *in the next interlude of seconds is seen looking up at the Manet illustration on the wall – shot of her, then of the illustration, then of her once more.*)

MISS MCLEOD: (*Thoughtfully*) Maybe you *will* go? – to Paris?
(*The viewer hears, but* MISS NESBIT *does not.*)

MISS NESBIT: I'm sorry – ?
(MISS MCLEOD *smiles, gives a barely perceptible shake of her head, allows the remark to be lost. . .*)

MISS MCLEOD: What are you doing now?

MISS NESBIT: I might get some odds and ends.

MISS MCLEOD: It seems very early. To go home, I mean.
(*Pause – with just a hint of nervousness at her own daring.*)
We could walk over to the Art Galleries. If you like.

MISS NESBIT: (*Worriedly; looks down at her feet*) I haven't really got the shoes –

MISS MCLEOD: (*Masking disappointment*) Oh. It doesn't matter.

MISS NESBIT: No. (*Looks up*) No. I should like that.

MISS MCLEOD: (*With concern*) But your feet –

MISS NESBIT: (*With a trace of desperation?*) It doesn't matter. Really. (*Pause.*) We *should* go.

MISS MCLEOD: '*Should* go'?

MISS NESBIT: It's there. All that 'culture'. Your friend Alistair told you about it. Now you can tell *me*. (*Pause.*) I've never used it at all. I'd like to.

MISS MCLEOD: It's very Scottish to want to employ your time usefully.

MISS NESBIT: I 'pass', do I?
    (*Pause – exchange of smiles between the two women.*)
MISS NESBIT: (*Casting an eye round the surroundings*) I don't *need* to
    go to Paris now. With all this. What would I do with Piss–
MISS MCLEOD: (*Interrupting*) Your cat?
MISS NESBIT: Pissarro.
MISS MCLEOD: It *is* a very odd name. For a cat.
MISS NESBIT: (*Momentarily forgetting discretion*) 'Pissarro' by
    name . . .
MISS MCLEOD: Oh – Dorothy!
    (*The two women exchange wry smiles.*)
MISS NESBIT: (*Confiding*) You know, Jean, I wasn't looking
    forward to the winter. Just the sales. Now it's going to be a
    – a very *useful* winter for me. Yes – an education.

EXT. ART GALLERIES: DAY 2
(*We view* MISS MCLEOD *and* MISS NESBIT *arriving at the Art
Galleries.*)
MISS NESBIT: (*Voice over*) If I had a wider fitting –
MISS MCLEOD: (*Voice over*) I'm sorry?
MISS NESBIT: (*Voice over*) My shoes. Americans don't have
    broad feet. So *we* shouldn't have broad feet either. That's
    how people's minds work.
MISS MCLEOD: (*Voice over*) Is it too far?
MISS NESBIT: (*Voice over*) I'll manage. Thank you. You just
    can't get the fittings, that's all. No one tries. If you're not
    the size you're supposed to be, they don't care.

INT. ART GALLERIES (FRENCH IMPRESSIONISTS' ROOM):
DAY 2
A WOMAN *passes* MISS MCLEOD *and* MISS NESBIT.
MISS NESBIT: (*Decisively*) Lanvin.
MISS MCLEOD: Pardon?
MISS NESBIT: (*Looking over her shoulder*) The scarf. I recognized
    it.
MISS MCLEOD: (*Fastening on paintings*) There're quite a few Van
    Goghs. He was friendly with a Glasgow dealer.

(MISS NESBIT *peers in general direction of the picture. Shot of*
MISS MCLEOD *walking towards the screen where it hangs.*)
Alexander Reid.
(*Shot of* MISS NESBIT *finding seat. She sits down. Handbag
placed on lap. Eases off one shoe: it doesn't come off completely,
but hangs from her toes.* MISS MCLEOD *looks backwards. She
sees, smiles. She leaves the painting, walks over, sits down.*)
(*Sympathetically, with genuine concern*) Footsore?
MISS NESBIT: I'm just taking it all in.
(MISS MCLEOD *nods her head, then casts an eye around at the
paintings.* MISS NESBIT, *sitting beside her, is taking critical note
of her companion.*)
Can I ask you something, Jean?
(MISS MCLEOD *hears, seems a little startled, either by the
enquiry or by the use of her name. Smiles cautiously, which* MISS
NESBIT *takes as her cue.*)
Why do you wear that brooch?
MISS MCLEOD: My brooch? (MISS MCLEOD *has a habit of
fingering her brooch; Miss Nesbit's remark causes more of the
same. She speaks patiently, defensively.*) I've always worn it. It
was a present.
MISS NESBIT: From – your man friend?
MISS MCLEOD: (*Following the lead; perhaps she's been about to say
something else in reply*) From Alistair.
MISS NESBIT: (*Nodding*) Who showed you the pictures?
MISS MCLEOD: (*Also nodding*) Yes. Alistair – Caird.
MISS NESBIT: (*Smiles cautiously*) If you don't mind my saying so
– Jean – it doesn't really 'go'.
MISS MCLEOD: 'Go'?
MISS NESBIT: Scarves look more – youthful – if they're knotted.
(*More tactfully.*) I hope I can say that to you?
MISS MCLEOD: (*Momentarily disorientated*) Yes. Yes, you can. It's
just – I'm used to a brooch. *This* brooch.
MISS NESBIT: (*Nodding*) For sentimental reasons?
MISS MCLEOD: I used to wear it to teach, you see.
MISS NESBIT: (*Observing the brooch critically*) It's like a charm, I
suppose, isn't it?

MISS MCLEOD: (*Skating around that deception*) I don't – well, you want to be *neat*. I've never been a very fashion-y person. I had to wear a black gown to teach in.

MISS NESBIT: (*Knowingly*) Black's the chic-est colour of all, of course.

MISS MCLEOD: Teaching's a very *chalky* job. It didn't matter so much what I had on underneath.

MISS NESBIT: (*Finally, conclusively*) Well, it's all 'appearances'. How you project yourself. You taught boys: I dressed their mothers.

(*Pause – both women notice a couple of* SCHOOLGIRLS. *The adolescents whisper and in turn are watching the women.*)

MISS MCLEOD: I couldn't have coped with girls, I don't think. They're wilier than boys. More treacherous. (*Pause – confiding.*) I had a friend once.

MISS NESBIT: The one up in the Mearns? In her hieland hame?

MISS MCLEOD: Miss Davie? No, before her. Long before. Someone I did my teacher training with. Her name was Nancy Colvin. (*Telling pause. Shrugs.*) I *thought* she was my friend.

(*Pause.*)

MISS NESBIT: (*Eyes narrowing shrewdly*) Alistair?

MISS MCLEOD: Yes. How did you guess?

MISS NESBIT: In 'business' it was a hen-house. I could tell from the tone in someone's voice.

MISS MCLEOD: It's silly after all these years. You don't forget, though.

MISS NESBIT: Was she pretty, your 'friend'?

MISS MCLEOD: (*Pursing her lips*) Not very. She was determined, though.

MISS NESBIT: (*More brightly, romantically*) Ah! She wished she could be in *your* shoes?

MISS MCLEOD: (*Without implied criticism of Alistair. She seems to be remembering her original 'confusion' of that time*) Alistair and I used to come and look at pictures. Like this. Exactly like this. I once saw her here, on her own – boning up, I suppose. Another time she followed us. Me and Alistair.

That was a bit – spooky. 'Oh look who it is,' Alistair said,
and he didn't sound very surprised, 'it's Nancy Colvin.'
(*Pause –* MISS MCLEOD *is thoughtful, ruminative.*)
(*Her face carries an odd expression of 'illumination'.*) They
sent me a postcard. From Paris. 'From Nancy and Alistair',
it said. 'Love from Nancy and Alistair'. They were on their
honeymoon.

MISS NESBIT: Oh, I'm sorry.

MISS MCLEOD: It was a postcard of the Palais-Royal. Near the
Tuileries. Where Colette lived.

(MISS NESBIT's *eyes narrow again. Are they wholly believing?*
MISS MCLEOD *stands up and walks slowly on.*)
I think that was the worst thing they could have done,
Dorothy, sending me that postcard. Even worse than
deceiving me – betraying me.
(*Pause while* MISS NESBIT *rises to her feet and follows* MISS
MCLEOD.)

MISS NESBIT: (*In her St Joan of Arc voice*) I know all about
betrayal. (*Preparing herself to glory in the account.*) For years
my father deceived my mother. Then he left her. For his
'other woman friend'. I used to think my mother should
have fought for him, to get him back. He was a very –
alluring man. Suave, good looking. None of the young men
I ever met was like him. I wished they could be.
(*Pause. The two women walk on very slowly.* MISS NESBIT
basing herself on film and television actresses she's seen, MISS
MCLEOD *looking solemnly between the paintings and* MISS
NESBIT.)
I saw them once in Regent Street. My father and his lady
friend. She was in a red dress. He must have bought it for
her. I followed them for blocks. Then they got into a black
taxi and sped off. I never saw them again. My father – and
his fancy piece in the red dress.
(*Pause. They are beside a woman's portrait, beneath glass.*)

MISS MCLEOD: Did you ever think *you'd* marry?

MISS NESBIT: (*Inspecting her appearance*) I wanted to look my
best for myself – not for men. (*She imposes a deliberate,*

significant pause.) Of course . . . (*Breath of a sigh.*) That always comes into it.

MISS MCLEOD: What does?

MISS NESBIT: Sex.

MISS MCLEOD: (*Unsurely; but not as shocked as we might have expected*) How?

MISS NESBIT: (*Mysteriously*) It comes into everything, doesn't it?
(*Pause. In the background we catch sight of a* COUPLE, *arm-in-arm. The* SCHOOLGIRLS *continue to perambulate.*) Would you still have taught if you'd married? Or started a family?

MISS MCLEOD: (*Considers, looks away*) Well, I had my boys.

EXT. ART GALLERIES: DAY 2

MISS NESBIT: Did you never want to teach girls?

MISS MCLEOD: (*Shrugging*) I started teaching boys. Boys are simpler. They don't give you problems. Not *those* problems anyway – growing up.

MISS NESBIT: What age were they?

MISS MCLEOD: Eleven, twelve.

MISS NESBIT: I should have thought you'd had plenty of problems.

MISS MCLEOD: (*With no evidence of criticism*) It's a man's world, isn't it?

MISS NESBIT: (*Defensively*) That's not *our* fault. Well, I was my own boss, virtually, at 'business' – so it was different for me. It's men who complicate women.

EXT. RIVER KELVIN: DAY 3

MISS MCLEOD *and* MISS NESBIT *are walking along the riverbank.*

INT. KELVINGROVE ART GALLERIES: DAY 4
(*Mix to*)
MISS MCLEOD *and* MISS NESBIT *in the Flemish Gallery.*
(*Mix to*)

EXT. HUNTERIAN MUSEUM: DAY 5
MISS MCLEOD *and* MISS NESBIT *are looking at sculptures.*

EXT. GEORGE SQUARE, EVENING: DAY 6
MISS NESBIT *and* MISS MCLEOD *are standing in George Square looking at Christmas decorations.*
MISS NESBIT: Our Santa Claus was sacked from the store one Christmas. Smoking on the job, they said. I think he'd had his hand in the till, too.

INT. PATISSERIE: DAY 7
MISS NESBIT *and* MISS MCLEOD *sit huddled over their cups of coffee. This is their 'refuge'.* MISS NESBIT *is airing another outfit: dress, coat, hat.*
MISS NESBIT: Do you keep up with any of your boys?
MISS MCLEOD: I don't – keep up – not exactly. I *know*, of course.
MISS NESBIT: Through the grapevine?
MISS MCLEOD: What I read – when I hear a name on the wireless.
MISS NESBIT: Famous ones?
MISS MCLEOD: Not really.
MISS NESBIT: (*Sounding unconvinced*) Oh. (*Pause. She draws on her cigarette, then crosses her legs. As much to herself.*)
It makes all the difference.
MISS MCLEOD: (*Absently*) Does it?
MISS NESBIT: Decent legs. I saw a photograph of Dietrich the other day. And she's older than us.
(*Pause.*) She was in – 'Shanghai Express', was it? – on television.
MISS MCLEOD: I don't watch films much. I like nature programmes. And art programmes – there was one on the Burrell Gallery.
MISS NESBIT: Of course, dear, that's your 'thing', isn't it? Art?
(*Pause.*)
You had your eyes opened for you, didn't you?
(MISS MCLEOD *looks puzzled.*)
I mean, your friend – Alistair – he taught you about paintings. How to 'see'.

MISS MCLEOD: Yes. I suppose he did. I was – very lucky.
(MISS NESBIT, *in her turn, seems puzzled by* MISS MCLEOD's *reserve on the matter*.)
MISS NESBIT: Can you remember it all?
MISS MCLEOD: I've read a lot since. In books, art books. I remember *that*.
MISS NESBIT: You didn't need to go to the art master, then. (*No response from* MISS MCLEOD.) In your school. (MISS MCLEOD's *further puzzlement*.) Like Miss Jean Brodie. Her romance.
(*Pause*.)
Really Alistair was *your* art master, wasn't he?
(*Pause*.)
MISS MCLEOD: (*Evasively*) In a way.
MISS MCLEOD: It's cold today. It's going to snow. (*She shivers*.)
MISS NESBIT: Someone walked over your grave?
(MISS MCLEOD *looks taken aback by the comment. Then she realizes it's a harmless remark. She smiles. Suddenly she changes tack*.)
MISS MCLEOD: (*Hopefully*) Still, we *could* have an outing. (*More cautiously*) If you'd like – ?
MISS NESBIT: Where to?
MISS MCLEOD: The Burrell, I wondered. I haven't been. And – Pollok House.
MISS NESBIT: (*Brightening*) Make it our winter entertainment?
MISS MCLEOD: We could take a taxi over.
(*Pause. Doubt crosses* MISS NESBIT's *features; then her face clears slightly*.)
MISS MCLEOD: There would be two of us. Just this once. Go Dutch?
(*Smiles exchanged: conspirators' smiles*.)

EXT. POLLOK HOUSE: DAY 8
A CHILD *is playing in the gardens of Pollok House.*

INT. POLLOK HOUSE: DAY 8
MISS MCLEOD *and* MISS NESBIT *by the El Greco painting of a
young woman in a fur collar.* MISS NESBIT *looks to painting:* MISS
MCLEOD *looks to* LITTLE GIRL *at the gate.*
MISS MCLEOD: She's very pretty, isn't she?
MISS NESBIT: (*Adjusting her fur collar*) Yes.
MISS MCLEOD: When I was a child I dreamed of wearing furs.
   (*They move off.*)

EXT. GARDENS OF POLLOK HOUSE: DAY 8
MISS NESBIT *and* MISS MCLEOD *are walking on the gravel beds on
the park side of the house; miniature box hedges. A* CHILD *is
running round and round inside the little knot garden.*
MISS MCLEOD: Wasn't there a maze in *Alice Through The
   Looking Glass*? I'm sure there was. Why should I remember
   that?
   (*Pause.*)
MISS NESBIT: Were you an imaginative child?
MISS MCLEOD: (*Lucidly: the far memory being very clear to her at
   this moment*) Some nights I used to dream I was lost in a
   maze. I walked round and round and round. I wasn't
   allowed to run. A sign said 'It is forbidden to run'. I could
   never find the way out. I knew there *must* be a way out,
   because I'd got in: how else could I have been there?
   (*Pause. Then, attempting a quite serious answer.*) All children
   are imaginative. It's later you lose that – gift.
MISS NESBIT: Did your boys lose it?
MISS MCLEOD: They went into the senior school.
MISS NESBIT: (*Pursuing her point*) But they lost their
   imagination?
MISS MCLEOD: In the senior school they became different.
   Grown up.
MISS NESBIT: Before they grew up, though, they were
   imaginative *then*? Before they'd stopped being children?
MISS MCLEOD: They didn't look like children, some of them.
   Their bodies 'matured'. But they hadn't lost – I don't know
   what it was. Curiosity. I don't mean they didn't fidget and

they weren't bored. But when they were interested, they gave their enthusiasm *back* to you. That was the best thing that ever used to happen.

(*Suddenly, after that revelation, we should see* MISS MCLEOD *as worn and fragile and slow – as we haven't quite seen her before. She pauses on the gravel.* MISS NESBIT, *ever solicitous of her own appearance, doesn't realize at first; then she does, and she halts. There's a few seconds' delay – and a kind of tension for us as we detect a dependence between the two women. In Miss Nesbit's next remark, do we find an attempt to cover over the fact of her companion's faltering progress?*)

MISS NESBIT: It's walking, that's the problem. I used to have a lot of walking, in the store. It's finding the shoes –

MISS MCLEOD: I've a broad instep.

MISS NESBIT: I don't have any proper *walking* shoes.

MISS MCLEOD: *You* have lovely shoes.

MISS NESBIT: (*Looking at her shoes*) I bought up a lot when the store closed. Wholesale, minus discount. I used to have twenty-three pairs of shoes to walk out in.

MISS MCLEOD: Don't you mind wearing them on gravel?

MISS NESBIT: You've got to have 'standards'. Miss Nesbit's Second Rule. That was my job, at 'business'. I had to be an example. I showed them a woman should take care, you should make the most of yourself, *for* yourself.

INT. BURRELL GALLERY: DAY 8

MISS NESBIT *and* MISS MCLEOD *enter through doors. It's winter outside.*

INT. BURRELL GALLERY: DAY 8

MISS MCLEOD *and* MISS NESBIT *are seen in the light-filled corridor of grey carpet where the stained glass hangs. They pass under an archway.*

MISS NESBIT: Do you go to church?

MISS MCLEOD: Just to Communion now. You can miss a few before they start counting. (*Pause.*) Which church do *you* go to?

MISS NESBIT: I used to go, I used to see customers. I've just got
out of the habit. As the ex-nun said.
(*Pause. Both women's heads look upwards at the coloured glass.*)
Do you – believe it all?
MISS MCLEOD: I don't really believe it or not believe it. I used
to feel better for going on Sunday morning.
MISS NESBIT: Better? (*She follows* MISS MCLEOD's *wandering
attention.* MISS MCLEOD *is now studying the other spectators.*)
Who are you looking at?
MISS MCLEOD: I . . . I thought . . . He's . . .
MISS NESBIT: Do you know him?
MISS MCLEOD: Maybe. I . . .
MISS NESBIT: Who is he? A neighbour?
(MAN's *form disappears.*)
MISS MCLEOD: No. No, from school. I –
MISS NESBIT: You taught him?
MISS MCLEOD: I think he was one of mine. I'm sure I know his
face . . .

INT. BURRELL GALLERY: DAY 8
MISS NESBIT *and* MISS MCLEOD *are seen walking round the
gallery. Trees are visible through the windows.*
MISS NESBIT: Have I told you? About the two women on the
other side of the square? Where I live? You must come
some time . . . They're sisters. They must be well up their
seventies, anyway. Someone told me. Fifty years ago – their
parents had died, they were sharing a house – one of them
decided to get married. Maybe it was to spite the other one,
I don't know. Anyway, the 'Big Day' came. The sister
married – she was the younger one, I think – and the older
one looked on. The couple of newly-weds drove off. The
next morning, first thing, the bride came back, in a taxi,
with her suitcases. She didn't say anything about it to her
sister but just came in off the pavement. And they lived
together again, ever after – not always so happily, I dare
say. The one who'd married never saw her husband again,
she wouldn't even speak to him. Not once. Whatever'd

happened, she couldn't have cared for it. Or maybe she was just wanting to 'make her point', do you think? About having her independence?

(*Upstairs, the two women are seen from behind, moving past the Manets; sketches of two Parisian women.*)

MISS MCLEOD: It was a very strange way to do it.

MISS NESBIT: What happens *is* stranger than anything you can read about. (*Pause.*) It's funny – how *we* see eye-to-eye.

MISS MCLEOD: (*Looks at* MISS NESBIT) 'See'?

MISS NESBIT: Being able to tell each other. (*Pause.*) With our different experiences.

(*Simultaneously, the two women lower themselves on to a sofa. We should be able to glimpse the Manets.*)

MISS MCLEOD: Yes. (*Pause.*) Yes. It's rather reassuring.

(*The word 'reassuring' prompts* MISS NESBIT'*s surprise.*) To find it *now*, I mean. (*She struggles to find words.*) It's not an *easy* time. This age. Is it?

MISS NESBIT: Perhaps if everything stayed the same, it would be. If you could keep your old friends. (*Pause – She considers.*) We wouldn't have met then.

MISS MCLEOD: No. That's what I meant. It's reassuring to know your – well, things don't just *end*. (*She stands up.*) There's another road – and corners to come –

INT. BURRELL GALLERY: DAY 8

MISS NESBIT *and* MISS MCLEOD *are among the glass cases: coffers, Egyptian heads, sarcophagi, Chinese burial urns. Behind the women, the* MAN *we've previously glimpsed – 30-ish – cruises into the background.*

MISS MCLEOD: (*The words are coming easily to her now*) Do you read Thomas Hardy?

MISS NESBIT: Not recently. I saw *Far from the Maddening Crowd* on television. With Julie Christie. Very interesting face, strong features.

MISS MCLEOD: Hardy said, as well as a birthday we each must have our 'death-day'. He didn't mean, when we die – but the anniversary of that day. Before it happens.

MISS NESBIT: I suppose we must have. If you think about it like that.
MISS MCLEOD: It could even be the same as your birthday. Your 'death-day'.
(*Pause.*)
MISS NESBIT: I think I prefer the paintings.
MISS MCLEOD: Why?
MISS NESBIT: Everything else has to do with death. Dying.
MISS MCLEOD: They're beautiful things, though.
(*Pause. We watch their faces through the glass cases: the women are framed in the glass, perhaps seen from a number of reflecting angles as they inspect the treasures. Behind them (maybe up in a first-floor gallery) we glimpse the predatory* MAN.)
I want to be buried. Beneath the ground. Somewhere like Tayvallich. Above the beach, looking out to sea.
(*Confidentially.*) Do *you* want to be buried?
MISS NESBIT: (*Very bluntly*) What's the choice? Buried or burned?
MISS MCLEOD: (*Awed*) Cremation – ?
MISS NESBIT: (*Retracting*) When I'm in the 'packaging' room I don't suppose it matters. Six and half a dozen.
MISS MCLEOD: (*Carefully, thoughtfully, so we remember the moment*) I know *I* want to be buried. Beneath the turf. With a stone on top of me. An old, mossy stone.
(MISS NESBIT'*s attention is arrested by what another woman is wearing. Adjusts collar in side of glass case.*)
Have you – ever wished – you'd had a child?
MISS NESBIT: (*Looking taken aback; then recovering, speaking very emphatically*) A child's only a claim parents make on each other.
(*Pause.*)
We said, 'No, thank you.' 'We'll have our independence, thank you.' A gift beyond price. That's how it was.
(*Pause.*)
MISS MCLEOD: (*Seen – again – as suddenly frail, vulnerable, cold*) I think – I'd like to go home now.
MISS NESBIT: I think my feet have had enough too!

(*Slowly* MISS MCLEOD *walks away.* MISS NESBIT, *with a last look at her reflection, follows.*)

EXT. MAIN DOOR OF BURRELL: DAY 8
MISS NESBIT *and* MISS MCLEOD *walk through the front doors. One door is held open for* MISS NESBIT *by the* MAN *we've glimpsed inside the building, whom* MISS MCLEOD *believes she's taught. He's with a* MALE FRIEND *– obvious and unmistakable indications of affection between them.* MISS MCLEOD *notices; her face threatens to cave in.* MISS NESBIT *doesn't see: she's too busy attending to her appearance (and now smoking?), lifting her shoes to inspect her heels for wear and tear.*

EXT. TAXI OUTSIDE CHURCH: DAY 8
MISS NESBIT *and* MISS MCLEOD *uncurl themselves from the back of the taxi. No one holds the door open.* MISS MCLEOD *appears cold and uneasy.* MISS NESBIT *seems unwilling to let the day finish quite so soon.*
MISS NESBIT: We could have a little something to see us
    home – ?
MISS MCLEOD: (*Ill at ease*) Perhaps I should go back. I have to
    go – (*Points in a vague direction.*)
MISS NESBIT: (*Taking the hint, retracting*) Yes, well, we've had
    our treat, haven't we? If it's going to snow – you said –
MISS MCLEOD: You'll be at the patisserie? Will you? On
    Wednesday?
MISS NESBIT: Unless it snows. I've no shoes, you see. For
    snow. Slush. I'll phone you and tell you if I can't.
MISS MCLEOD: I don't –
MISS NESBIT: (*Surmising the wrong conclusion – perhaps because
    she wants to believe it?*) You don't have a phone?
MISS MCLEOD: (*Repeating her: not initially meaning to say it but
    enticed into the untruth*) I don't have a phone. No.
MISS NESBIT: (*Looking round*) Maybe the weathermen have got
    it wrong.
MISS MCLEOD: (*Anxiously*) Then I'll see you on Wednesday? At
    the same time?
MISS NESBIT: At the same time.

MISS MCLEOD: Well . . . (*Achieves a smile.*) It *was* a treat, wasn't it? Just how you said. 'A treat.' *Your* word.
(MISS NESBIT *smiles hazily, uncertain about having the term attributed to her. Behind them both is the stained glass of the church.* MISS NESBIT *seems to be holding on to the moment: she casts a professional eye over* MISS MCLEOD, *who appears uncomfortable, cold, distracted.*)
MISS NESBIT: You really should try pastels. I could give you a scarf. They'd suit your colouring. And just something round your eyes, a smidgen.
MISS MCLEOD: I'm not sure about that.
MISS NESBIT: It's just an idea.
MISS MCLEOD: I'm sure you know.
(*Pause. A different kind of awkwardness from the initial one: an unsureness about how 'personal' they should be.*)
I'll go along the terrace. I'm up behind –
MISS NESBIT: I go the other way. I'll walk down Byres Road.
MISS MCLEOD: (*Concerned*) Is it quite safe?
MISS NESBIT: There are police cars about.
MISS MCLEOD: Oh.
MISS NESBIT: (*Trying to say the 'right thing'*) I hope it *doesn't* snow.
MISS MCLEOD: So do I.
MISS NESBIT: The Gardens slope. It's the bother with the pavements, they're like an ice-slide.
MISS MCLEOD: Goodnight Dorothy.
MISS NESBIT: Goodnight Jean.

INT. MISS MCLEOD'S FLAT: DAY 9
Library film of 1981's winter storms and blizzards.

INT. MISS MCLEOD'S FLAT: DAY 9
Stretched mirror shot: Miss McLeod's window – through it she is seen pallidly. Light goes out – only reflection of snow is visible.

INT. PATISSERIE: DAY 10
MISS NESBIT *sitting alone in patisserie.*
WAITRESS: Another coffee, madame?

MISS NESBIT: No, thank you.

WAITRESS: Where is your friend today?

MISS NESBIT: We missed a week. We said we wouldn't come if it snowed, but I thought perhaps with the thaw . . .

WAITRESS: The snow has been terrible, perhaps *next* week.
(MISS NESBIT *lifts the* Glasgow Herald *– sees death notice – registers shock.*)

EXT. STEPS OF CREMATORIUM: DAY 11

Opening shot of MISS NESBIT *in appropriately black coat and turban and gloves, à la Elizabeth Taylor. 'Miss McLeod's Party' is indicated on a signboard behind her.* MISS NESBIT *is standing on top of a flight of steps. The door opens.* MRS BLACK *walks out. She, too, is wearing some very respectable, rather expensive, funeral attire.* MISS NESBIT *half turns round.*

MRS BLACK: Miss Nesbit?

MISS NESBIT: Yes.

MRS BLACK: (*In friendly fashion*) I'm Jean's sister. Margaret Black. (*Momentary pause.*) We've heard about you from the lawyer.
(*The two black-clad women stand shaking hands.*)

MRS BLACK: It was so good of you to come. The roads up from Chester were awful. Roll on spring!

MISS NESBIT: (*Rather blankly; maybe for 'something to say'?*) You live in Chester?

MRS BLACK: We were always on at Jean to come down and see us. She never would, of course. You know Jean. She 'didn't want to give us any bother'. (*Smiles forgivingly.*) What a case! That was just her, wasn't it?
(*Pause – during which* MRS BLACK *rubs her gloved hands. Seeing* MISS NESBIT'*s seriousness, her smile feels less comfortable, although she persists.*)
We've been in Chester for twenty years now. We went for my husband's job. Brian hasn't managed up . . .
(*Pause –* MISS NESBIT *gives a disbelieving little smile and nod.* MRS BLACK *vaguely looks round for inspiration: she's a hale and capable person, normally given to mending holes in*

*any conversation. If they start walking now – down the steps
and on to gravel – it would provide an echo of the Pollok
House exchange.*)

MRS BLACK: I think Jean would have liked the service. We
wanted a good crematorium. It's – simplest like this, isn't
it?

MISS NESBIT: (*Cautiously rather than rudely*) It wouldn't be
everyone's choice. Do you think – do you think she *knew*?

MRS BLACK: '*Knew*'? It was all so sudden.

MISS NESBIT: (*Working through her own mental associations*) The
last time I saw her, she talked about the death-day. When
we went to the Burrell.

MRS BLACK: (*At a loss*) The 'death-day'? I don't understand –

MISS NESBIT: She'd read about it. In – Thomas Hardy. Some
writer. He said we have a death-day – as well as a birthday.
Only we don't know when it is.

MRS BLACK: (*Taken aback*) Oh. I see.

MISS NESBIT: (*Repeating herself*) Yes. You see, the last time I
was with Jean we went to the Burrell, we saw all the things.
We had a very pleasant afternoon. It was very educational.
She knew a lot about art.

MRS BLACK: Jean did?

MISS NESBIT: Yes. Jean.
(MRS BLACK *smiles, not quite so confidently as before.*)
(*Looking round*) I thought – there might have been a few
more here. Some of her pupils maybe. Or her friend, from
the school, Miss – (*Tries to remember.*)

MRS BLACK: Miss Davie?

MISS NESBIT: Yes.

MRS BLACK: She saw it in the papers. She wrote to me.

MISS NESBIT: She lives up north somewhere.

MRS BLACK: The Mearns. Yes, it's been hell up there with the
storms. Even worse than we've had it down south. I'm sure
Jean would have understood why she didn't come. You
have to be practical, don't you? At our age?
(*Pause – it's an uncomfortable one for* MISS NESBIT.)
(*Laying a hand on* MISS NESBIT'*s elbow.*) Look, I've got to

go back to Jean's flat now. There's lots to sort through –
will you help me, Miss Nesbit?
(MISS NESBIT *hesitates at the request; then nods.*)

INT. MISS MCLEOD'S FLAT: DAY 11
The flat is in the process of being 'cleared'. MRS BLACK *and* MISS
NESBIT *are in the bedroom. We see a packing case or two, and some
cardboard boxes. There's a bed, a table beside it and a wardrobe
with a mirror.*
Hanging from the lintel of the wardrobe is the coat MISS MCLEOD
*has always worn, with brooch fixed to the lapel. It seems to slouch
from its wooden yoke.* MRS BLACK *already has her coat off, and her
sleeves are pulled back in a businesslike fashion. She's sorting
through a pile of clothes – woollens – packing or discarding. There
are two cardboard boxes near her to receive them.*
MRS BLACK: (*Lifting up some jumpers*) Oxfam'll take these,
    won't they? (*More quietly, as much to herself.*) I don't think
    they'd fit *me*. (*Looks over at* MISS NESBIT.) Either of us.
    Jean never ate enough –
    (*Pause.* MRS BLACK *peers into the boxes on top of an upturned
    packing case. She looks over, sees the other woman's
    awkwardness. She smiles at her, forgets about the jumpers for
    the moment. She speaks in an intimate-sounding voice.*) The
    lawyer's told you about the money, of course?
MISS NESBIT: (*Slowly*) Oh yes . . .
MRS BLACK: It'll be a nice little nest-egg, won't it? But – we'd
    like you to have something as well. Something of Jean's. To
    keep. A memento.
MISS NESBIT: (*Obviously surprised*) I – don't know. That's –
    very kind of you.
MRS BLACK: (*In benign tone of voice*) Is there anything you can
    think of?
    (*MISS NESBIT turns her head, looks round. Her attention is
    suddenly caught by the telephone. She stares at it and appears to be
    transfixed for a few seconds.* MRS BLACK *leans forward to see.*)
MISS NESBIT: (*As if weighing the words; a statement, but balanced
    like a question*) She *had* a phone?

MRS BLACK: (*More confidentially*) Yes. Didn't she try to ring
    you?
MISS NESBIT: No.
MRS BLACK: (*With a shake of her head*) Why didn't she ring?
    Ring *someone*? I don't understand.
MISS NESBIT: Oh . . . Jean was very – independent.
    (*Pause.* MRS BLACK *looks from* MISS NESBIT *to the telephone,
    then to the pile of clothes in her hand. She begins sorting again,
    holding the garments against herself and folding them or
    relegating them.*)
MRS BLACK: (*Rather more as a courtesy than from active interest*)
    How – how did you and Jean meet?
MISS NESBIT: (*Recovering a little*) By chance, I suppose. (*Relief
    of words, we feel.*) Then we went to look at paintings. We
    visited the galleries. She knew a lot about art, you see.
    (*Pause –* MRS BLACK *nods, she's heard the bones of the
    account before, at the crematorium.*)
    She'd heard it from someone. I believe he once meant a
    great deal to her. (*Pause.*) Alistair.
MRS BLACK: (*With surprise, her curiosity aroused*) Alistair?
    Alistair who? Do you know?
MISS NESBIT: (*Struggling to remember*) She did tell me. 'Craig'.
    No, that wasn't it. 'Caird' – I think. Yes, 'Caird'.
MRS BLACK: Alistair Caird? (*Shakes her head.*) Well, well, *there*'s
    a name from the past!
MISS NESBIT: (*Re-appropriating* her *story*) I believe she –
MRS BLACK: (*Picking up the threads of a different story*) One of
    the skeletons in my cupboard! We used to go out together.
    We were practically engaged –
MISS NESBIT: (*With an expression of shocked dismay*) *You* – went
    out with him?
MRS BLACK: (*The story tumbles out*) Oh yes. Until he took a shine
    to one of my friends. One of our crowd. I must have pined
    for – oh, all that spring! (*Smiles.*) Then – one evening I was
    introduced to Brian – and we just hit it off. I had my happy
    ending after all! (*Blithely.*) Alistair Caird! Fancy Jean
    remembering that. I'd almost forgotten him!

MISS NESBIT: But I thought he married . . . someone Jean had done her teacher training with?

MRS BLACK: (*Laughs again*) Goodness, Nancy wouldn't have lasted a day learning to teach!

MISS NESBIT: (*Anxiously*) Was that Nancy Colvin?

MRS BLACK: Yes. (*Laugh fades a little.*) Yes, that's right. The *name*'s right.
(*Pause –* MRS BLACK *lifts a petticoat from the top of a pile of underwear. She looks at it very critically. Then starts to fold it elaborately.*)

MISS NESBIT: (*Incredulous*) Nancy Colvin married your friend Alistair – and you didn't mind?

MRS BLACK: (*Laughs*) No. (*She deposits the petticoat in a cardboard box. Picks up another, and in the course of the conversation sifts through several petticoats and vests and pairs of knickers.*) Mind you, Jean probably didn't approve. Sometimes she was a bit too hard on people. I was at their wedding. Maybe they didn't invite Jean, I can't remember.

MISS NESBIT: (*After a short delay, during which we see her trying to assimilate all this latest information*) Jean said – they sent her a postcard from Paris.

MRS BLACK: A postcard – to *Jean*?

MISS NESBIT: They were in Paris on their honeymoon. Alistair and Nancy.

MRS BLACK: *Were* they? I don't remember that. (*Pause.*) *I* was in Paris on my honeymoon. With Brian. Maybe Jean was thinking –

MISS NESBIT: You're sure?

MRS BLACK: (*Less comfortably*) About Paris? (*Awkward laugh.*) Yes, of course. We stayed near the Luxembourg Gardens.

MISS NESBIT: We talked about Paris, you see. Jean seemed very sure. She told me about your grandfather, the artist. When *he* was in Paris –

MRS BLACK: Our grandfather? An artist? You must be mistaken –

MISS NESBIT: (*Slowly*) Jean didn't have a grandfather who painted?

MRS BLACK: (*As pleasantly as she can manage*) Well, I'm her sister – he was *my* grandfather too!

(MISS NESBIT *looks crestfallen.* MRS BLACK *is sensitive enough to realize.*)

(*Half-jokingly*) Not unless our grandfather was a *secret* painter! (*Pause. Considerately, seeing* MISS NESBIT'*s mounting puzzlement and distress.*) Look, I think Jean just got confused. She got her stories muddled. Alistair was *my* 'beau', not hers. Maybe she wanted Alistair to notice her, and he didn't. I don't know. (*She picks up another item of underclothing, folds it; continues to address* MISS NESBIT, *who's still perched on the edge of the bed.*) You see, Jean was very 'retiring', let's say. She preferred to watch, from the sidelines. Watch life. (*Pause.* MRS BLACK *picks up school gown.*) Do they wear these any more? (*She rolls the gown into a bundle, hesitates where to put it; drops it into one of the cardboard boxes.*) Right! (*Places hand on top of clothes in one of the cardboard boxes.*) That's all Oxfam! What's next?

MISS NESBIT: (*Simply, helplessly*) So how did she know? All about Paris?

(MRS BLACK *turns her attention to a pile of stockings/ handkerchiefs/scarves/gloves on the bed, beside* MISS NESBIT. *In the course of her search, we should recognize a scarf previously worn by* MISS MCLEOD.)

MRS BLACK: Paris?

MISS NESBIT: Yes. We used to talk about Paris.

MRS BLACK: (*Sees* MISS NESBIT'*s condition; feigns enthusiasm*) Have you been?

MISS NESBIT: (*Barely attending*) No. No, I haven't.

MRS BLACK: You *should*. You could go now, couldn't you? With the money. Your windfall. Give yourself a treat? Maybe that's what Jean meant it for? You'd love Paris. Brian and I –

MISS NESBIT: Yes, your honeymoon –

MRS BLACK: Well, we've been back a few times since then. (*Pause.*) You *could* go, couldn't you? Get away?

MISS NESBIT: Now? In winter?

MRS BLACK: No, wait till the better weather. April in Paris.
You'd love it.
MISS NESBIT: (*Nods*) I *could* go –
MRS BLACK: There's nothing to keep you, is there? No pet?
MISS NESBIT: (*With a ghost of a smile*) No, not even a cat.
(MRS BLACK *smiles, not understanding her insistence on the
point.*)
I might have had one, a cat. I thought about it. Someone in
the store – in millinery – she had kittens to give away. She
gave them silly names. Rather *rude* names.
MRS BLACK: (*Cajoling*) You could get one. If you'd like to. You
could give it whatever name you wanted.
MISS NESBIT: They're a lot of trouble.
MRS BLACK: Oh no, cats are excellent company. Brian and I
have two. (*Pause.*) I'd think about it, I really would.
MISS NESBIT: Yes, I could call it 'Pissarro'.
MRS BLACK: (*Laughs unsurely*) Yes. (*Pause.*) But first things
first. You need a holiday. Why not go? – To Paris? You do
look a wee bit peaky, if you don't mind me saying so. It's
the weather, we could all do with a change of scene. All the
business with Jean. Get out of your dark clothes. What's to
stop you? (*Pause.*) You could see – oh, so much. The Left
Bank. The Tuileries Gardens. All the galleries. You'd like
that.
MISS NESBIT: (*Slightly dazed*) Yes.
MRS BLACK: (*Ever practical*) Could someone go with you
perhaps?
MISS NESBIT: I'm all right on my own. I'm used to cities. (*Her
mind follows its own logic.*) I'm from London. Originally.
London way.
(*Pause.* MRS BLACK *considers the pile on the bed with a degree
of exasperation. Decides to dump it intact in one of the boxes.*)
MRS BLACK: (*Consulting her watch*) Look at the time!
(MISS NESBIT *holds up her wrist.*)
Did I ask you, Miss Nesbit – Brian and I were wondering
if there was anything of Jean's you'd like as a keepsake?
(MISS NESBIT *picks up her coat, rises from the bed and walks*

*across the room, towards the wardrobe. The coat is still
hanging.*)

MISS NESBIT: There's that brooch.

MRS BLACK: Yes. Of course. Take it. Did Jean tell you about it?

MISS NESBIT: (*Unpinning the brooch as she speaks*) It was a
present. She liked to wear it – for sentimental reasons –
someone special gave it to her –

MRS BLACK: (*Relieved, seeing an end in sight to their exchange*) It
was a retirement present. From the boys. I always thought
it was a little heavy myself. Rather – *solid*. I'm sure Jean
would have loved you to have it. We think you should have
something, a memento –

MISS NESBIT: (*Digesting the revelation*) Did you say, a retirement
present?

(MRS BLACK *takes down the overcoat. Lifts the brooch from*
MISS NESBIT's *palm, has a last look at it.*)

MRS BLACK: Yes. From the boys at school. Something for her to
remember them by. It was a nice thought, wasn't it?
(*Returns brooch to* MISS NESBIT's *hand, closes her fingers over
it. Encouragingly.*) There, have it! (*Quickly looking round the
room.*) Well, I think I've done all I can here for the moment
(*Walking towards the door.*) I'll just get my things, then we
can go.

(MISS NESBIT, *still without her coat, remains by the wardrobe
door, studies herself. Her own coat is over one arm. She pins the
brooch to it; puts on the coat. Talks to herself in the mirror.*)

MISS NESBIT: (*Addressing her reflection*) The woman in the red
dress: I told that story about 'Father's Woman' so often, I
honestly believed it. There was no red dress, and there was
no woman. My father died quite young. The doctor told us
his clockwork had run down; that was all.
(*During next remark,* MRS BLACK *re-enters room. She halts
when she sees, hears.*)
Where we lived, in Norwood, no one wore red. (*Realizes
she's been overheard. For a second or two, she stares – then
laughs. Her laugh is embarrassed, apologetic, alive to the
situation.*) My mother used to shake her head at me. 'You've

too much imagination, Dorothy Nesbit, that's your trouble.
Too much imagination.'
(MRS BLACK's *response is also to laugh, rather nervously.*)
But if you don't have *that* – what *do* you have?
MRS BLACK: (*Businesslike suddenly. Pleasantly hectoring tone, but
shaking flat's keys*) A holiday, Miss Nesbit, that's the
answer. Do think about it. I'm sure Jean would have
wanted it. Paris isn't so far.

EXT. TRAVEL AGENCY: DAY 12
MISS NESBIT *is wearing either her funeral coat or a similarly dark
one. The brooch is missing. A large poster of Paris is displayed in the
travel agency window.* MISS NESBIT *enters the agency, then exits
holding brochures. She is wearing reading glasses. She walks along
Byres Road, still holding brochures.*
MISS NESBIT: *You* should have gone, Jean. (*Pause – stunned
realization.*) We shouldn't have said we'd never been.
(*Walks towards a bin on a lamp-post and dumps the literature.
Takes off her glasses and puts them in her handbag.*)

EXT. CAMPUS, GIBSON ST: DAY 12
We follow MISS NESBIT's *brisk progress to a dress shop.
Background of 'French' chanteuse-style music. 'Paris Originals' are
advertised in the window, alongside a 'Sale' notice.* MISS NESBIT *is
seen inside the shop, through glass. In the next shot* MISS NESBIT
*exits, wearing her old coat but with the new red dress visible beneath.
She's holding a carrier bag; a shop-name, 'French Leave', is printed
on the gold- or silver-coloured plastic.*

EXT. PATISSERIE: DAY 12
MISS NESBIT *approaches along the opposite pavement of Byres
Road.*

INT. PATISSERIE: DAY 12
WAITRESS: (*To* MISS NESBIT) Bonjour.
(*A* WOMAN *occupies Miss McLeod's chair.* MISS NESBIT
approaches the table. The WOMAN *is in her fifties, more smartly*

dressed than MISS MCLEOD *and 'better preserved'. She's also less 'self-involved' than either of the older women.*)

MISS NESBIT: May I?

WOMAN: (*Politely*) I'm sorry?

MISS NESBIT: Share?

WOMAN: (*Obligingly, very willingly*) There's not much room I'm afraid.

(*Pause, while* MISS NESBIT *removes her coat and settles. She keeps her hat on. There's a startling contrast between the sober hue of her coat and the brilliant red of her new dress. The* WOMAN *hands menu across the table.* MISS NESBIT *takes it, puts it down without looking at it.*)

MISS NESBIT: I don't have my reading glasses. (*Calls across to* WAITRESS *at counter.*) Café au lait, s'il vous plait. Pour moi. (*To* WOMAN) It's expensive, but it's worth it.

(MISS NESBIT *looks at* WAITRESS, *who takes a long draw on her cigarette and appears distinctly cool. During the following, the carrier bag is perfectly obvious to us. We have the feeling that* MISS NESBIT *isn't really partaking in the following exchange – she's working on automatic pilot, and it's the* WOMAN *who's 'carrying' the conversation.*)

(*Turning to the* WOMAN, *scarcely lowering her voice*) She's French, I believe. Parisian.

WOMAN: Is she? I'm sorry – (*Admiringly*) – I've been looking at your dress.

MISS NESBIT: *It's* French too. I bought it in Paris.

WOMAN: It's lovely. Such a cheerful colour. For winter. Cherry red. (*Pause.*) I wonder why we pick one colour and not another.

(*Pause.* MISS NESBIT *lights a cigarette, plants it in her holder.*)

MISS NESBIT: (*With less solicitude than at beginning of play*) You don't mind?

(WOMAN *tilts her head questioningly.*)

MISS NESBIT: If I smoke?

WOMAN: (*Pleasantly*) No. Do –

MISS NESBIT: It's not a *vice*, not really.

WOMAN: No.

MISS NESBIT: (*Sounding a little weary of the line*) A *treat*. To hell with the expense!
(*Pause.* MISS NESBIT *blows out smoke.*)
WOMAN: I suppose this place is just like Paris.
(*Pause.*)
MISS NESBIT: Don't you think it is?
WOMAN: I've never been to Paris.
MISS NESBIT: You haven't really lived.
WOMAN: My husband – he died recently – he always said we should go. We just never got round to it.
MISS NESBIT: Your family?
WOMAN: No. There was only ourselves. (*Pause.*) But *you've* been?
MISS NESBIT: To Paris? Yes, a few times. There's a silver light there. My grandfather was an artist, he trained to paint there.
WOMAN: How interesting!
MISS NESBIT: What an eccentric! He had a grey bushy beard.
WOMAN: It's the sort of place I feel – it sounds ridiculous – you *know* Paris: even though you haven't been there. Don't you think so?
MISS NESBIT: I'm thinking of going again. I've a cat, though.
WOMAN: Couldn't someone take her in? Look after her for you?
MISS NESBIT: 'Pissarro'. It's a 'he'. A tom.
WOMAN: Oh.
MISS NESBIT: It's a lot of trouble. Maybe I'll go.
WOMAN: (*Brightly*) Well, thinking about it, that's half the pleasure, isn't it? What you *might* do.
(*Pause.* MISS NESBIT *casts the* WOMAN *an enquiring look.*)
(*Clarifying.*) Just thinking about it. (*Pause.*) There's a psychological explanation, I expect. Perhaps my husband and I never went to Paris because we were afraid we'd be disappointed. Do you think?
(MISS NESBIT *is blowing out cigarette smoke – lots of it.*)
It's all in the mind.
(MISS NESBIT *hurriedly stubs out her cigarette, looking at her watch.*)

The subconscious acting –

MISS NESBIT: I've forgotten an appointment. You'll have to
    excuse me.

WOMAN: (*With some disappointment*) Oh.

MISS NESBIT: (*Calling over*) No coffee, waitress, please.

WAITRESS: Madame?

MISS NESBIT: (*Rising to her feet*) I have an appointment. An
    important appointment.

WAITRESS: (*From counter*) No coffee? You want something else?

MISS NESBIT: (*Looking at girl, putting on her coat*) No thank you.
    Merci.

WOMAN: Perhaps – another time?

MISS NESBIT: (*Turning her attention from the* WAITRESS) I'm not
    normally in here.

WOMAN: Maybe we could –

MISS NESBIT: Our paths may cross.

WOMAN: (*After* MISS NESBIT *has collected her belongings,
    including the carrier bag*) Well . . . Goodbye. It's been very
    nice talking –

MISS NESBIT: (*Unenthusiastically*) Yes. (*She doesn't dally.*) Au
    revoir, they say, in Paris.

WOMAN: (*Repeating her*) In Paris?

MISS NESBIT: For 'goodbye'.

WOMAN: Au revoir . . .

    (*A sultry, sulky pout from the* WAITRESS. *She replaces cup and
    saucer, returns to cigarette, leafs through the pages of* Elle.
    MISS NESBIT *makes for the door.*)

EXT. PATISSERIE: DAY 12

MISS NESBIT *contemplates the life passing on the street. She is not
without pathos, finally; nor without a curious kind of confidence. A
woman's mode of dress catches her eye, and she turns her head over
her shoulder; she follows her with her gaze. One of those inimitable
French songs of endurance rings out.*

PRIVATEERS
A short story

'Up' or 'down' was Miss Armitage's dilemma, do I move up the house or down?

'Down' she decided at last, into the basement. (Call it a 'garden flat', it sounded better.) That way she'd be spared the heat in summer through the roof tiles. From the windows beneath the railings and street level she would be able to keep a watch on who went in and out of the house, her lodgers and their friends.

So the removal men came and Miss Armitage made her retreat downstairs. As much as possible was crammed into the warren of small rooms. She hardly had room to turn, there was so much furniture (inherited from her parents, mostly) and every surface so crowded with knick-knacks. But Miss Armitage didn't think of the awkwardness, even when her elbow banged on a cabinet door or against a table, or when her hand sent an ornament flying. Instead she pictured her furnishings and gewgaws in the surroundings that to her mind became them best: not here in the basement, nor in the dark and modest, suffocating rooms of the house upstairs, which had been her parents' – but in large, light-filled rooms, in superior houses, her objects the possessions of people she chose to think now had been her friends, in the long-ago days when she'd still believed, hope against hope, that the world might be Alice Armitage's oyster.

In the little sitting-room of the basement tea is already waiting on a tray. The cups are fine bone china. The tray is laid with a cloth embroidered with Alpine flowers. The tea is Orange Pekoe. Some packet biscuits are fanned on a plate. Miss Armitage has put out the good Hester Bateman silver teaspoons, one in each saucer, and a third in the sugar bowl.

The young man who rings the doorbell, always on cue, is Mr Finch. He talked about himself once, but Miss Armitage has more or less forgotten all he said. He occupies two rooms on the second floor: at the back of the house, because he is a fellow (Miss

Armitage believes he may have mentioned) of limited means. However, he is smartly turned out each time he comes to see her for tea, in a charcoal flannel suit, and he wears his hair short, which is how Miss Armitage considers young men ought to look. She appreciates his courteous attention to his appearance. He may have told her what his line of business is: but she has seen him sometimes from her scullery window in the middle of mornings and afternoons, wearing his other, very modern 'casual' clothes as the newspapers call them, so she thinks his occupation must be one which allows him quite a bit of free time.

He is very polite, Mr Finch, as Miss Armitage wishes everyone in the world would allow themselves to be. He always sits where she bids him to sit. 'I'm so glad you could come,' she invariably says by way of welcome; but the surprise in her voice is unnecessary because these twice-weekly afternoon tea visits are a custom, they've been taking place for several months, she forgets just how long.

Miss Armitage forgets a lot, of what is current and here-and-now and to do with the house and its running, and of what appears in the newspapers and on the television set, which she prefers (most of the time) to keep covered with a tartan rug. But there is another life inside her head, containing the version of the past she keeps specifically for these afternoon teas, and in that respect she has excellent 'recall'.

Some word or thought will act as a trigger, and the mechanism is activated. Mr Finch has to do nothing except sit and listen, sip his tea and nibble at a biscuit and hear his hostess embark on her major and minor re-adjustments of the past.

In the stories she offers to her favoured lodger, Alice Armitage is quite a humdinger of a young woman. She goes to dances and her mother shows her off, her two older sisters pass on their diplomatic advice on the one great subject, 'Men'. She is lunched, wined and dined, and taken to tea-dances; she spectates at Cowes from the bow of a yacht, she watches the polo mounts from the stand at Hurlingham.

Her life as she reconstructs it in those other decades is gracious and thankfully hemmed in with all manner of social ritual.

In her basement, her 'garden flat', Miss Armitage no longer has on show the framed photographs of her family, now all delivered to their Maker in the hereafter. The photographs have been relegated to the gloom of drawers, locked from view; the too familiar faces are forbidden from sharing in the splendour of Miss Armitage's accounts because she knows they wouldn't understand, not without the gift of imagination they were lacking in life, their expressions wouldn't show her any sympathy.

Yet her intentions are only of the best. In her (revised) version of the past her father receives the reward that was due to him – he doesn't just manage, he *owns* the muslin works; her mother doesn't lose her fine looks, they don't fade, and she continues to draw the eyes of handsome strangers across crowded public rooms; her sisters are given the alternative husbands they always deserved to have, an MP and a Harley Street surgeon, both with prominent social connections.

Miss Armitage explains to her teatime caller that why she herself didn't marry was owing to a positive embarrassment of offers, because she couldn't decide in the end which one of all her suitors she should make her graceful surrender to and accept.

The speaker's attention occasionally returns to the young man in the charcoal suit seated opposite her, she focuses – but as if from yards away, not feet – on her Mr Finch from upstairs.

He smiles, sips his tea, and looks appreciatively round the over-furnished sitting-room.

When Miss Armitage is especially tired and that past time she has been telling her visitor of is making a ringing in her ears – so that she feels she's under one of the glass bell-jars on the mantelpiece – at that point she'll grant a nod of dispensation, like a duchess, and the young man will rise to his feet, then begin his customary perambulation of the room.

Miss Armitage is aware, vaguely – as she lies back in the chair and closes her eyes, opens them blearily, closes them again – she is aware of what Mr Finch is about. She realizes that her memory, or the lack, isn't wholly responsible for the little losses of things that she keeps making in the course of the week: a teaspoon, a paperweight, a piece of ivory, the silver letter-opener, the wee jade dragon from China. With the *things*, because they belong to the perfect past she has collected around her, her mind *is* engaged and doesn't let slip, it remembers, records. She isn't the one to blame this time, not entirely.

Nor, she thinks, is the culprit, Mr Finch, who's sometimes her only visitor between one afternoon tea and the next in the week. Occasionally she thinks that she sees something sorrowful in his face, and that that's why he gives her his time and listens to her, because his own life has not been the most satisfying sort, he too has had his chances but they've been snatched away at the last moment. She recognizes that look, it makes her sad for him.

Leaning back and with her eyes closed, Miss Armitage continues her story, her stories, of her desirable, imagined past. Country weekends and London jaunts, picnics and riding to hounds. She remembers what the ladies wore as she stood and watched them, from the careful distance she was required to observe; she recalls word-perfectly the exchanges among the men as she homed in and listened, from her discreet and respectful distance, as they drank from stirrup cups on frosty mornings or studied the form of the sculls on the river.

Somewhere nearby, in the sitting-room of her basement, Miss Armitage also hears the young man: engaged in his deft, light-fingered work. He never interrupts her, he lets her polish and refine her details, arrange her stories as she wishes them to be. He is very considerate, very quiet. Her Mr Finch.

She cares to think he is not like some of the other tenants in the house, clumping up and down stairs and playing their records too loudly and sending bathwater gushing from the overflow. Discretion and consideration have gone to the four winds apparently, and Miss Armitage is very sorry about it. But Mr Finch offers her back silence, and tact, and a kind of submission that gratifies her heart.

It doesn't even matter about the bits and pieces that are here one day and gone the next. Anyway, Miss Armitage knows, their life and purpose belong elsewhere. She was left the majority of her possessions in relatives' wills, and while the objects have been with her she has given them more 'appropriate' histories than those they had. In the days when she went out for walks she used to pass antique and bric-à-brac shops and it would occur to her that no one can know a blind thing about what sits in these windows: their pasts are secrets, you buy something and it's up to you to *give* it its history.

Or perhaps it was the other way about, she'd started to think of late, since her move downstairs into the basement: really the object owns *you*, and discovers its new owner whenever *it* feels the need of another life.

He always lets himself out, Mr Finch, and so quietly that she hardly even hears the soft clicking shut of the door.

Miss Armitage sits on over the gas fire, she dozes maybe. Usually her caller has brought her something, a gift: a few flowers, a half-pound carton of chocolates. She smells the flowers from her armchair, anticipates the taste of the chocolates. She imagines a garden seen somewhere, over a fence or a hedge or in a magazine; she tries to remember the name of a 'chocolatier' whose window she used to stand looking into, once upon a time, when the streets of London had style. In her mind's wanderings she's been admitted to the garden, she's a guest at a weekend party, everyone is waiting to say 'hello' to her; or a man, a square-cut handsome man, is buying her chocolates in the shop with the white marble walls and floor – a whole box of chocolates, and asking to have it wrapped in gold foil and tied with red ribbon.

At another level of consciousness Miss Armitage knows that upstairs the house is filling again with its young, throbbing life. A different sort of noise may cause her to jump, she hears footsteps passing up on the street, keys or a stick being rattled along the area railings. Sometimes – so she remembers – when she's been up and about on her feet and has twitched the net curtain back, the person she's seen hasn't been any of the other faceless and nameless ones who belong to the transient company of Number Twenty-Eight, Belvedere Street. She'll have chanced to catch a glimpse of her Mr Finch, not in his nice suit but dressed in his 'casual' clothes, and he'll have had his arm around someone, the same person every time, an up-to-the-minute young woman with a mane of frizzy carrot hair. Whenever it's happened, the two of them have been laughing together, laughing their heads off.

Miss Armitage supposes that it is love, the lucky couple's happy abandon – timeless love. Safe and secure again in the familiar hold of her old, worn armchair, she spares kind thoughts for all in their situation, imagining to herself the glorious, blissful adventure love must be.